The Dragon

a play by Joy Cowley

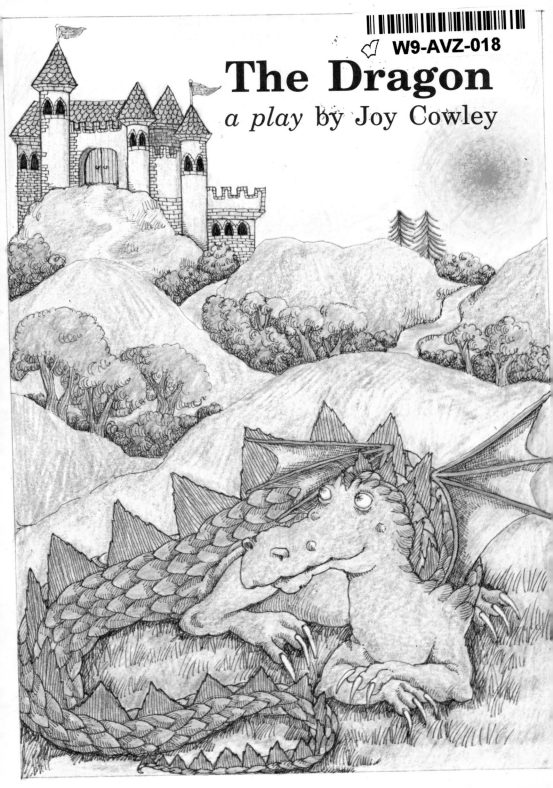

King

Sir Tim

Frog

Princess

Dragon

2

King:

Sir Tim, I want you to help me.

Sir Tim:

What is it, your majesty?

King:

I want you to get rid of
the dragon.

Sir Tim:

I can't, your majesty.

Not that dragon.

It huffs and puffs fire.

King:

I'll let you marry the princess.

4

Sir Tim:

I'd rather not, your majesty.
I'd like to marry a princess,
but—but—

King:

But what?

Sir Tim:

I don't want to get cooked,
your majesty.

Frog:

Hey, King, I can help you.

King:

Who said that?

Sir Tim:

It's a frog, your majesty.

King:

So it is.
Can you help me, Frog?

Frog:

Yes, O King.

I can put out the dragon's fire.

King:

Then I'll give you a bag of gold.

Frog:

I'd rather marry the princess.

King:

All right.
You put out the dragon's fire,
and the princess is yours.

Frog:

I'll do it right away.
Right away, O King.
Hey, Dragon! Where are you?

Dragon:

Roar, roar!

Frog:

There you are, old chimney.
See if you can catch me.

Dragon:

Roar! Huff, puff, roar!

Frog:

Come on, Dragon. This way.

Sir Tim:

Look! The frog is going
to the river.

King:

The dragon is
going after him.

Sir Tim:

The frog has jumped
into the water.

King:

And there goes
the dragon.
What a splash!

Dragon:

s-s-S-S-S-S-s-s-s.

Sir Tim:

His fire is out, your majesty.

12

Frog:

See? I said I could do it.
Now, where's the princess?

Princess:

I'm here. But I'm not
going to marry a frog.

King:

You have to, my dear.

Princess:

I will not!

Frog:
Hey! *You* can't be
a princess.

Princess:
Oh, can't I?
I *am* a princess,
so there!
And I don't
like frogs.

Frog:
But you are ugly.

Princess:
What? You broken-down old frog!
You're the one who's ugly.

Frog:

It's time for me to go.
Goodbye, King.

King:

Where are you going?

Frog:

As far away as I can.

Sir Tim:

But what about the princess?

Frog:

I'd rather marry the dragon.
You can have her, Sir Tim.
She's all yours.
Goodbye! Goodbye!

Sir Tim:

Wait, Frog. Wait!
Not so fast!
I'm coming, too.

16